This book belongs to

_____

WALT DISNEY
VOLUME 16

LI'L WOLF
SAVES THE DAY

WALT DISNEY FUN-TO-READ LIBRARY

ISBN 1-885222-28-9
Advance Publishers Inc., P.O. Box 2607, Winter Park, FL. 32790
Printed in the United States of America
098765432

One day, Big Bad Wolf went for a walk through the woods.

He was doing what he liked to do best. He was thinking about pigs.

"Yum-yum!" said Big Bad Wolf. "How I do love pigs! Pork chops! Bacon! Ham! If only there were an easy way to catch pigs!"

PIGS' COUNTY FAIR

SUNDAY

Just then he saw a sign on a tree. "As I live and breathe!" said Big Bad Wolf. "It is time for the Pigs' County Fair!"

Big Bad Wolf heard a sound behind him. Someone was coming down the road. "A wolf like me cannot be too careful," he said. "I will hide until I see who that is."

Big Bad Wolf hid behind a tree. He was just in time. The Three Little Pigs were walking down the road. Li'l Wolf was walking with them.

Practical Pig was the first to see the sign about the fair. "How great!" he cried. "The County Fair!"

"The fair was lots of fun last year," said Fifer Pig.

"It will be even more fun this year," said Fiddler Pig. "This year <u>we</u> will win the three-legged race."

"No races for me," said Practical.
"This year I will make preserves. No pig
in the county makes better preserves than
I do. I'll be sure to win a prize!"
      The Three Little Pigs ran off to get ready.
Li'l Wolf went along to help.

Big Bad Wolf came out of hiding. He smiled a wolfish smile.

"Wonderful!" he said. "The Three Little Pigs will be at the fair. They will be having so much fun, they will forget to watch out for me. That's when I'll catch them!

"And this will show that son of mine how to be a <u>real</u> wolf!"

Then Big Bad Wolf went on his way. He rubbed his hands with glee.

The Three Little Pigs did not think for a moment that Big Bad Wolf might come to the fair. In fact, they did not think of him at all. Practical was busy making his preserves.

Fiddler and Fifer were busy too. They
had to practice for the three-legged race.
Li'l Wolf helped them.

"Ready, set, go!" cried Li'l Wolf. He was happy to help Fiddler and Fifer practice.

Then it was Li'l Wolf's turn. "I will enter the potato-sack race," he said. He hopped back and forth all day.

Fiddler and Fifer timed him to see how fast he hopped.

After he practiced, Li'l Wolf ran to the
store. He got sugar for Practical's preserves.
He got spices and flour, too. Practical also
wanted to bake some pies. "My pies are even
better than my preserves," he said.

Practical rolled out the pie crusts. Fiddler
and Fifer helped. They all tasted the pie
filling. And when the pies were finished, they
licked the bowl.

On the day of the fair, the four friends set out early. They brought the pies and the preserves. Li'l Wolf brought his sack.

But when they got to the fairgrounds, the stout pig at the gate would not let Li'l Wolf in. "You are not a pig!" he said. "You are different. We do not want you here!"

"But Li'l Wolf is our friend!" said Practical.

"He worked hard to get ready for the fair!" said Fifer.

"And he helped us to get ready, too," said Fiddler.

"Only pigs are allowed," said the guard. "And he is not a pig. He cannot come in."

"Well, then we won't go in either," said
Practical.

"But you must!" cried Li'l Wolf. "If you
don't, who will tell me about the fair
afterward?" Then sadly Li'l Wolf walked away
from the fair.

"The pigs do not want me at the fair," he
thought. "And my pop is always cross with
me because I am not a big bad wolf like he
is. I don't fit in anywhere."
Li'l Wolf began to cry.

Suddenly he heard someone coming. It was someone who laughed a mean and hungry laugh.

Li'l Wolf stopped crying. He peeped out from behind a bush. There he saw his pop. Big Bad Wolf was carrying a sack. He was headed toward the fairgrounds.

"I can't miss!" said Big Bad Wolf. "All
the pigs in the county will be in one place.
I'll come home with a sack full of piggies!"
"Golly!" said Li'l Wolf. "I had better
warn the pigs before my pop gets to the fair."

Li'l Wolf ran off. He took a shortcut
across the fields. He ran as fast as he could.
He was out of breath when he got to the fair.

The stout and grumpy pig at the gate would still not let him in.

"Practical!" shouted Li'l Wolf. "It's me! My pop is coming! Watch out!"

The guard heard what Li'l Wolf said. Maybe he would let Li'l Wolf into the fair after all.

"Don't be afraid, Li'l Wolf," said Practical. "Your pop will not catch any pigs today. We will take care of everything."

"Yes, you go right in and enjoy the fair," said the guard.

Li'l Wolf went in and walked around. He knew Practical would make sure all the pigs were safe from Big Bad Wolf.

Practical hurried away to make a trap. Some of the other pigs helped. Together they built a small wooden shack. Then they made a hole just big enough for Big Bad Wolf's head.

When they were all done, they ran and hid.

When Big Bad Wolf came to the fair, there was no guard to keep him out. There was only Li'l Wolf. He was practicing for the sack race.

"Bah!" said Big Bad Wolf to himself.
"That kid is a disgrace to wolfdom. He is
not even trying to catch any pigs. Well, as
soon as I fill my sack, I will have to teach
him a thing or two!"

Big Bad Wolf walked around. He did not see a single pig anywhere. "Where can they be?" he wondered. "This is the Pigs' County Fair. They must be here somewhere."

Then Big Bad Wolf saw the shack. And
he saw a sign that said Piggies in Here.
"Aha!" said Big Bad Wolf. "I can't wait to
get my hands on those pigs!"

Practical popped out from behind a bush.
He slammed the door of the shack. The door
pushed Big Bad Wolf right smack into the
back of the shack.

Big Bad Wolf's head squeezed right
through the hole. Practical's trap had worked!

"Help!" Big Bad Wolf cried. "Get me out of here!"

The pigs popped out from behind trees and bushes. "No wolves allowed at the fair!" they shouted.

"Except for Big Bad Wolf," said Fiddler.
"He can stay," said Practical. "He can be
a part of the fair."

And the pigs did make Big Bad Wolf part of the fair. They held the First Great Pie-Throwing Contest. Big Bad Wolf was the target.

The other pigs joined Li'l Wolf on the
other side of the fair. They let him hop in the
sack race. And Li'l Wolf won first prize.

Later that day Practical spoke up. "We must always remember how Li'l Wolf saved us," he said. "He warned us that Big Bad Wolf was coming!"

The other pigs cheered for Li'l Wolf.

They lifted him to their shoulders. They carried him around the fairgrounds. "You will always be welcome here," they told him. "You are our friend. Friends are welcome no matter how different they are."

When the fair was over, all the pigs
went home. They left Big Bad Wolf covered
with pies.

On his way home, Practical told Li'l Wolf about the joke they had played on Big Bad Wolf. He knew that Li'l Wolf would go back for his pop and help him home. That was just the kind of wolf Li'l Wolf was.